CW00958473

# DON'T DRINK THE PINK

**OTHER BOOKS BY THE SAME AUTHOR:**

*The Grumpface*
*Henry and the Hidden Treasure*
*Titch the Itch*
*Don't Ever Look Behind Door 32*
*The Day That A Ran Away*
*The World's Greatest Mousetrap*

**DON'T DRINK THE PINK**

B.C.R. Fegan

Cover art and illustrations by Lenny Wen

Published by TaleBlade Press

TaleBlade

www.taleblade.com

For Anaya - ever loved

# DON'T DRINK THE PINK

## B.C.R. FEGAN

### ILLUSTRATED BY
## LENNY WEN

TALEBLADE

Grandfather Gilderberry
never seems to rest.
He's always in his workshop,
working at his best.

Dad thinks he's crazy.
Mom thinks he's just old.
But I think he's amazing
and worth his weight in gold.

I like his crooked smile.
I like his croaky sound.
But what I like the best is
when my birthday comes around.

On my **first** birthday,
he came with a surprise.
He had a box of potions,
and a twinkle in his eyes.

"Happy birthday, Madeline,"
he said with a wink.
"Take a potion, take a brew.
Just don't drink the pink."

I think I had the **red** one.
I'm really not quite sure.
Mom says I was breathing fire
all about the floor.

On my **second** birthday,
Grandpa couldn't wait.
He woke me in the morning
of that very special date.

"Happy birthday, Madeline,"
he said with a wink.
"Take a potion, take a brew.
Just don't drink the pink."

I'm told I took the **blue** one,
though I wasn't quite awake.
I turned into a mermaid,
so they put me in the lake.

On my **third** birthday,
I waited by the door
until my Grandpa Gilderberry
came in like before.

"Happy birthday, Madeline,"
he said with a wink.
"Take a potion, take a brew.
Just don't drink the pink."

I know I took the **yellow**.
It gave me super speed.
I raced a locomotive,
and I quickly took the lead.

On my **fourth** birthday,
I woke up to the rain,
and as I finished breakfast,
my grandpa came again.

"Happy birthday, Madeline,"
he said with a wink.
"Take a potion, take a brew.
Just don't drink the pink."

I quickly took the **orange**,
and much to my surprise,
when I moved my arms about,
I controlled the skies.

On my **fifth** birthday,
I didn't have a clue,
but Mom invited all my friends,
and Grandpa, he came too.

"Happy birthday, Madeline,"
he said with a wink.
"Take a potion, take a brew.
Just don't drink the pink."

I passed around the **purple**,
and to my mom's dismay,
each and every one of us
were tiny for the day.

On my **sixth** birthday,
I woke up feeling great.
I wasn't even worried
when Grandpa came in late.

"Happy birthday, Madeline,"
he said with a wink.
"Take a potion, take a brew.
Just don't drink the pink."

I cautiously chose **green**,
but I knew I wasn't wrong
when that very tasty liquid
made me really, really strong.

On my **seventh** birthday,
Grandpa bounded in.
He wore a crooked smile
which broke into a grin.

"Happy birthday, Madeline,"
he said with a wink.
"Take a potion, take a brew.
Just don't drink the pink."

I sipped a little on the **brown**
and found that I could fly.
I guzzled down the rest of it
and soared into the sky.

On my **eighth** birthday,
I ran and didn't stop.
Before the sun had risen,
I had come to Grandpa's shop.

"Happy birthday, Madeline,"
he said with a wink.
"Take a potion, take a brew.
Just don't drink the pink."

I reached out for the **black** one
and drank till I was full.
Then slowly from my head to toes,
I turned invisible!

On my **ninth** birthday,
Grandpa took us to the sea.
He said he had a feeling
something big would come to me.

"Happy birthday, Madeline,"
he said with a wink.
"Take a potion, take a brew.
Just don't drink the pink."

I picked up the **white** one
and watched as people fled,
for I'd turned into a giant
with a massive giant's head.

On my **tenth** birthday,
I woke before the sun.
Grandpa threw a party
and invited everyone.

"Happy birthday, Madeline,"
he said with a wink.
"Take a potion, take a brew.
Just don't drink the pink."

When I sipped the **bronze** one,
I could build things with my mind.
I built a theme park for my friends,
with rides of every kind.

On my **eleventh** birthday,
I waited half the day,
before Grandpa hobbled in
like he had been away.

"Happy birthday, Madeline,"
he said with a wink.
"Take a potion, take a brew.
Just don't drink the pink."

I gently raised
the **silver**
and drank it with a cheer,
as every sip I took,
a new me would appear.

On my **twelfth** birthday,
Grandpa wasn't well.
He came by with his present
but decided not to dwell.

"Happy birthday, Madeline,"
he said with a wink.
"Take a potion, take a brew.
Just don't drink the pink."

I drank every bit of **gold**.
It tasted just like honey,
and anytime I clapped my hands,
they got filled up with money.

On my **thirteenth** birthday,
I went out for a walk
and stopped by Grandpa's shop
for presents and a talk.

"Happy birthday, Madeline,"
he said with a wink.
"Take a potion, take a brew.
Just don't drink the pink."

The one I chose was **clear**,
and I almost made Dad fall
when I ran home to surprise him
and could walk through any wall.

On my **fourteenth** birthday,
Grandpa looked quite frail.
I found him on a hilltop,
moving like a snail.

"Happy birthday, Madeline,"
he said with a wink.
"Take a potion, take a brew.
Just don't drink the pink."

I held up the **opal**,
and it sparkled in the sun,
and when I drank, I could hear
the thoughts of everyone.

On my **fifteenth** birthday,
Grandpa didn't come.
He'd passed away a month ago.
"He's resting now," said Mom.

"Happy birthday, Madeline,"
I said, and went outside.
I walked to Grandpa's workshop,
where I sat and thought and cried.

Through my tears, I looked up,
and there, right by the sink,
a note said, "Happy Birthday,"
and behind it was the **pink**.

I didn't understand,
but the note said, "Never fear."
I sipped the most delicious drink
and wished Grandpa was here.

And suddenly the whole room swirled
like water down a drain.
I felt myself get pulled through time,
and I was **one** again!

And there! My Grandpa Gilderberry,
much to my surprise.
He had a box of potions,
and a twinkle in his eyes.

"Happy birthday, Madeline,"
he said with a wink.
"Take a potion, take a brew.
Just don't drink the pink."

Lightning Source UK Ltd.
Milton Keynes UK
UKHW051325070220
358310UK00004B/116